708

ALLEN COUNTY PUBLIC LIBRARY

FRIENDS
OF ACPL

P9-CND-360

HOLIDAY COLLECTION

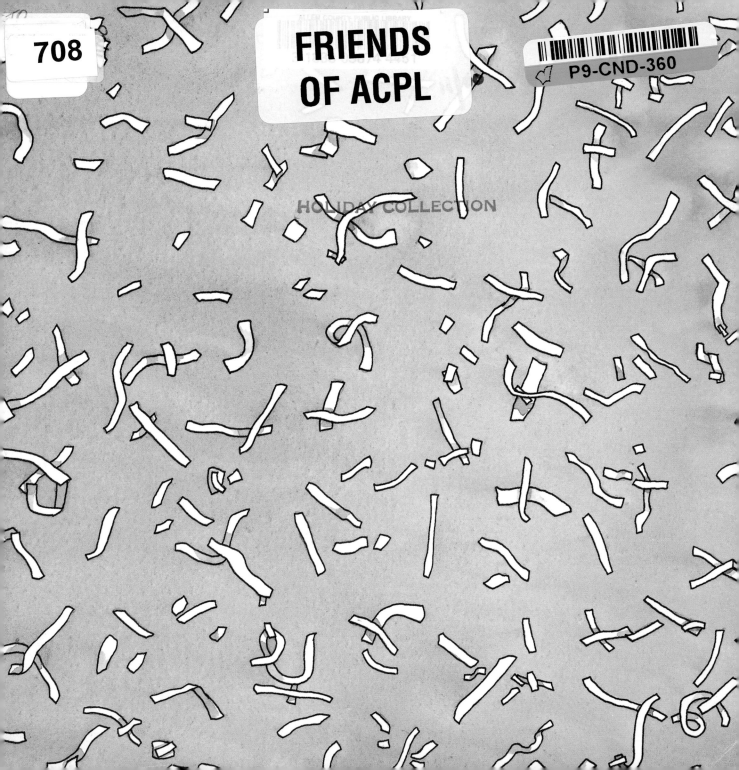

To my son John, a constant source
of joy and pride to his mother.

Copyright © 2000 by Sylvia Long. All rights reserved.

Book design by Susan Van Horn.
Typeset in Bernhard Modern and Papyrus. Printed in Hong Kong.
The illustrations in this book were rendered in pen and ink with watercolor.

Library of Congress Cataloging-in-Publication Data
Long, Sylvia.
Deck the hall : a traditional carol / by Sylvia Long.
p. cm.
Summary: An illustrated version of the classic Christmas carol celebrating "the season to be jolly."
ISBN 0-8118-2821-2
1. Folk songs, English—England—Texts. 2. Christmas music—Texts.
[1. Folk songs—England. 2. Christmas music.] I. Title.
PZ8.3.L8555 De 2000
782.42'1723'0268--dc21   00-008934

Distributed in Canada by Raincoast Books
9050 Shaughnessy Street, Vancouver, British Columbia V6P 6E5

10 9 8 7 6 5 4 3 2 1

Chronicle Books LLC
85 Second Street, San Francisco, California 94105
www.chroniclebooks.com/Kids

Deck the Hall

A Traditional Carol illustrated by Sylvia Long

chronicle books · san francisco

Allen County Public Library
900 Webster Street
PO Box 2270
Fort Wayne, IN 46801-2270

Deck the hall with boughs of holly,
Fa la la la la, la la la la.

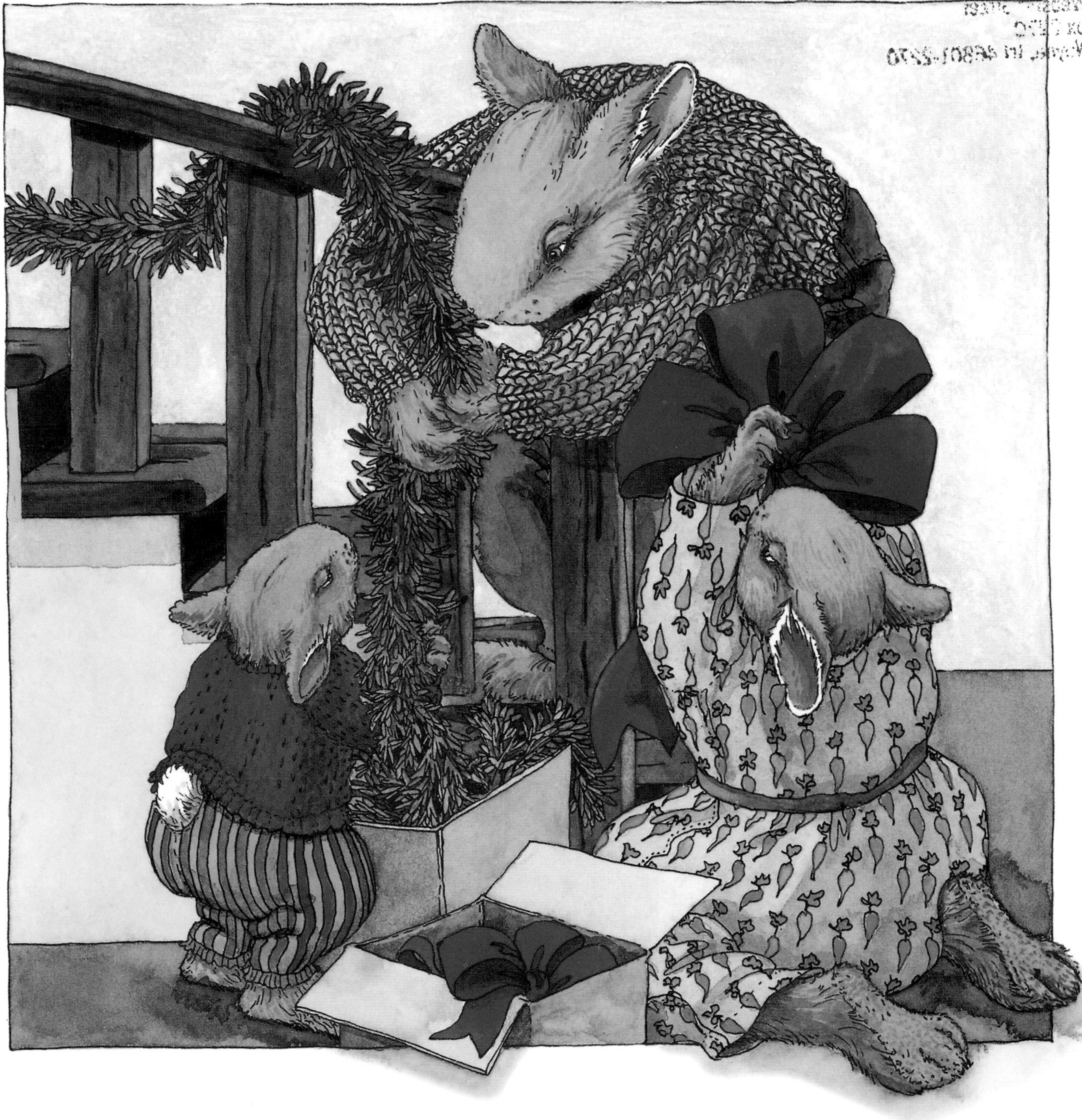

FA - LA - LA
LA -
LA -
LA -
LA -
LA - LA -
LA - LA

'Tis the season to be jolly,

Fa la la la la, la la la la.

FA - LA - LA - LA - LA - LA - LA - LA - LA - LA - LA - LA

Don we now our gay apparel,

Fa la la, la la la, la la la.

Troll the ancient yuletide carol.

Fa la la la la, la la la la.

See the blazing yule before us,
Fa la la la la, la la la la.

FA - LA - LA

Strike the harp and join the chorus,

Fa la la la la, la la la la.

Follow me in merry measure,

Fa la la, la la la, la la la.

While I tell of yuletide treasure.

Fa la la la la, la la la la.

FA - LA - LA - LA - LA - LA - LA - LA - LA - LA - LA

Fast away the old year passes,
Fa la la la la, la la la la.

FA - LA - LA

Hail the new, ye lads and lasses,
Fa la la la la, la la la la.

FA - LA - LA - LA -
LA - LA - LA - LA - LA

Sing we joyous all together,
Fa la la, la la la, la la la.

Heedless of the wind and weather.

Fa la la la la, la la la la.

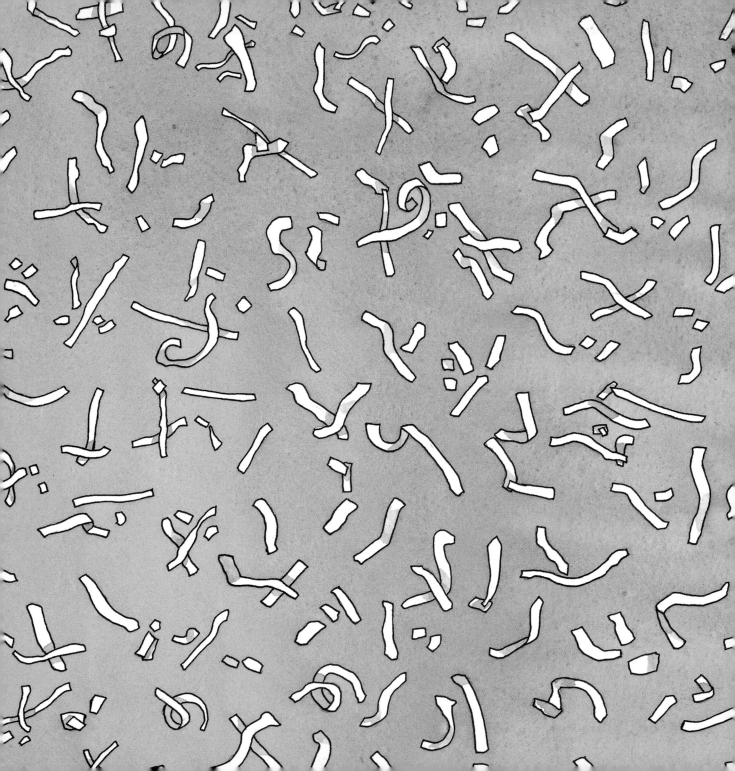